SENTRY OF THE SKY

SENTRY OF THE SKY

by Evelyn E. Smith

There had to be a way for Sub-Archivist Clarey to get up in the world—but this way was right out of the tri-di dramas.

Clarey had checked in at Classification Center so many times that he came now more out of habit than hope. He didn't even look at the card that the test machine dropped into his hand until he was almost to the portway. And then he stopped. "Report to Room 33 for reclassification," it said.

Ten years before, Clarey would have been ecstatic, sure that reclassification could be only in one direction. The machine had not originally given him a job commensurate with his talents; why should it suddenly recognize them? He'd known of people who had been reclassified—always downward. I'm a perfectly competent Sub-Archivist, he told himself; I'll fight.

But he knew fighting wouldn't help. All he had was the right to refuse any job he could claim was not in his line; the government would then be obligated to continue his existence. There were many people who did subsist on the government dole: the aged and the deficient and the defective—and creative artists who refused to trammel their spirits and chose to be ranked as Unemployables. Clarey didn't fit into those categories.

Dispiritedly, he passed along innumerable winding corridors and up and down ramps that twisted and turned to lead into other ramps and corridors. That was the way all public buildings were designed. It was forbidden for the government to make any law-abiding individual think the way it wanted him to think. But it could move him in any direction it chose, and sometimes that served its purpose as well as the reorientation machines.

SENTRY OF THE SKY

So the corridors he passed through were in constant eddying movement, with a variety of individuals bent on a variety of objectives. For the most part, they were of Low Echelon status, though occasionally an Upper Echelon flashed his peremptory way past. Even though most L-Es attempted to ape the U-E dress and manner, you could always tell the difference. You could tell the difference among the different levels of L-E, too—and there was no mistaking the Unemployables in their sober gray habits, devoid of ornament. It was, Clarey sometimes thought when guilt feelings bothered him, the most esthetic of costumes.

*

The machine in Room 33 extracted whatever information it was set to receive, then spewed Clarey out and sent him on his way to Rooms 34, 35, and 36, where other machines repeated the same process. Room 37 proved to be that rare thing in the hierarchy of rooms—a destination. There was a human Employment Commissioner in it, splendidly garbed in crimson silvet and alexandrites—very Upper Echelon, indeed. He wore a gold mask, a common practice with celebrities who were afraid of being overwhelmed by their admirers, an even more common practice with U-E non-celebrities who enjoyed the thrill of distinguished anonymity.

Then Clarey stopped looking at the Commissioner. There was a girl sitting next to him, on a high-backed chair like his. Clarey had never seen a U-E girl so close before. Only the Greater Archivists had direct contact with the public, and Clarey wasn't likely to meet a U-E socially, even if he'd had a social life. The girl was too fabulous for him to think of her as a woman, a female; but he would have liked to have her in his archives, in the glass case with the rare editions.

"Good morning, Sub-Archivist Clarey," the man said mellowly. "Good of you to come in. There's rather an unusual position open

6

and the machines tell us you're the one man who can fill it. Please sit down." He indicated a small, hard stool.

Clarey remained standing. "I've been a perfectly competent Sub-Archivist," he declared. "If MacFingal has—if there have been any complaints, I should have been told first."

"There have been no complaints. The reclassification is upward."

"You mean I've made it as a Musician!" Clarey cried, sinking to the hard little stool in joyful atony.

"Well, no, not exactly a Musician. But it's a highly artistic type of job with possible musical overtones."

Clarey became a hollow man once more. No matter what it was, if it wasn't as duly accredited Musician, it didn't matter. The machine could keep him from putting his symphonies down on tape, but it couldn't keep them from coursing in his head. That it could never take away from him. Or the resultant headache, either.

"What is the job, then?" he asked dully.

"A very important position, Sub-Archivist. In fact, the future welfare of this planet may depend on it."

"It's a trick to make me take a job nobody else wants," Clarey sneered. "And it must be a pretty rotten job for you to go to so much trouble."

The girl, whom he'd almost forgotten, gave a little laugh. Her eyes, he noticed, were hazel. There were L-E girls, he supposed, who also had hazel eyes—but a different hazel.

*

"Perhaps this will convince you of the job's significance," the interviewer said huffily. He took off his mask and looked at Clarey with anticipation. He had a sleek, ordinary, middle-aged-to-elderly face.

SENTRY OF THE SKY

There was an awkward interval. "Don't you recognize me?" he demanded.

Clarey shook his head. The girl laughed again.

"A blow to my ego, but proof that you're the right man for this job. I'm General Spano. And this is my Mistress, Secretary Han Vollard."

The girl inclined her head.

"At least you must know my name?" Spano said querulously.

"I've heard it," Clarey admitted. "'The Fiend of Fomalhaut,' they call you," he went on before he could catch himself and stop the words.

The girl clapped her hand over her mouth, but the laughter spilled out over and around it, pretty U-E laughter.

Spano finally laughed, too. "It's a phrase that might be used about any military man. One carries out one's orders to the best of one's ability."

"Besides," Clarey observed in a non-Archivistic manner, "what concern have I with your military morality?"

"He's absolutely perfect for the job, Steff!" she cried. "I didn't think the machines were that good!"

"We mustn't underestimate the machines, Han," Spano said. "They're efficient, very efficient. Someday they'll take over from us."

"There're some things they'll never be able to do," she said. Her hazel eyes lingered on Clarey's. "Aren't you glad, Archivist?"

"Sub-Archivist," he corrected her frostily. "And I hadn't really thought about it."

"That's not what the machines say, Sub-Archivist," she told him, her voice candy-sweet. "They deep-probed your mind. You don't do anything, but you've thought about it a lot, haven't you?"

Clarey felt the blood surge up. "My thoughts are my own concern. You haven't the right to use them to taunt me."

8

"But I think you're attractive," she protested. "Honestly I do. In a different way. Just go to a good tailor, put on a little weight, dye your hair, and—"

"And I wouldn't be different any more," Clarey finished. That wasn't true; he would always be different. Not that he was deformed, just unappealing. He was below average height and his eyes and hair and skin were too light. In the past, he knew, there had been pale races and dark races on Earth. With the discovery of other intelligent life-forms to discriminate against together, the different races had fused into a swarthy unity. Of course he could hide his etiolation with dye and cosmetics, but those of really good quality cost more than he could afford, and cheap maquillage was worse than none. Besides, why should his appearance mean anything to anybody but himself? He'd had enough beating around the bush! "Would you mind telling me exactly what the job is?"

"Intelligence agent," said Spano.

"Isn't it exciting?" she put in. "Aren't you thrilled?"

*

Clarey bounced angrily from his chair. "I won't sit here and be ridiculed!"

"Why ridiculed?" Spano asked. "Don't you consider yourself an intelligent man?"

"Being an intelligence agent has nothing to do with intelligence!" Clarey said furiously. "The whole thing's silly, straight out of the tri-dis."

"What do you have against the tri-dis, Sub-Archivist?" Spano's voice was very quiet.

"Don't you like any of them?" the girl said. "I just adore *Sentries of the Sky!*" Her enthusiasm was tinged, obscurely, with warning.

SENTRY OF THE SKY

"Well, I enjoy it, too," Clarey said, sinking back to the stool. "It's very entertaining, but I'm sure it isn't meant to be taken seriously."

"Oh, but it is, Sub-Archivist Clarey," Spano said. "*Sentries of the Sky* happens to be produced by my bureau. We want the public to know all about our operations—or as much as it's good for them to know—and they find it more palatable in fictionalized form."

"Documentaries always get low ratings," the girl said. "And you can't really blame the public—documentaries are dull. Myself, I like a love interest." Her eyes rested lingeringly on Clarey's.

They must think I'm a fool, Clarey thought; yet why would they bother to fool me? "But I am given to understand," he said to Spano, "even by the tri-dis, that an intelligence agent needs special training, special qualifications."

"In this case, the special qualifications outweigh the training. And you have the qualifications we need for Damorlan."

"According to the machines, all I'm qualified for is human filing cabinet. Is that what you want?"

Spano was growing impatient. "Look, Clarey, the machines have decided that you are not a Musician. Do you want to remain a Sub-Archivist for the rest of your days or will you take this other road? Once you're on a U-E level, you can fight the machines; tape your own music if you like."

Clarey said nothing, but his initial hostility was ebbing slowly away.

"I wanted to be a writer," Spano said. "The machines said no. So I became a soldier, rose to the top. Now—this is in strictest confidence—I write most of the episodes of *Sentries of the Sky* myself. There's always another route for the man with guts and vision, and, above all, faith. Why don't we continue the discussion over lunch?"

*

It was almost unthinkable for L-E and U-E to eat together. For Clarey this was an honor—too great an honor—and there was no way out of it. Spano and the girl put on their masks; the general touched a section of the wall and it slid back. There was a car waiting for them outside. It skimmed over the delicately wrought, immensely strong bridges that, together with the tunnels, linked the great glittering metropolis into a vast efficient whole.

Spano was not really broadminded. Although they went to the *Aurora Borealis*, it was through a side door, and they were served in a private dining room. Clarey was glad and nettled at the same time.

The first few mouthfuls of the food tasted ambrosial; then it cloyed and Clarey had to force it down with a thin, almost astringent pale blue liquid. In itself, the liquor had only a mild, slightly pungent taste, but it made everything else increasingly delightful—the warm, luxurious little room, the perfume that wafted from the air-conditioning ducts, Han Vollard.

"Martian mountain wine," she warned him. "Rather overwhelming if you're not used to it, and sometimes even if you are. . . . " Her eyes rested on the general.

"But there are no mountains on Mars," Clarey said, startled.

"That's it!" Spano chortled. "When you've drunk it, you see mountains!" And he filled his glass again.

While they ate, he told Clarey about Damorlan—its beautiful climate, light gravity, intelligent and civilized natives. Though the planet had been known for two decades, no one from Earth had ever been there except a few selected government officials, and, of course, the regular staff posted there.

"You mean it hasn't been colonized yet?" Clarey was relieved, because he felt he should, as an Archivist, have known more about the planet than its name and coordinates. "Why? It sounds like a splendid place for a colony."

"The natives," Spano said.

"There were natives on a lot of the planets we colonized. You disposed of them somehow."

"By co-existence in most cases, Sub-Archivist," Spano said drily. "We've found it best for Terrans and natives to live side by side in harmony. We dispose of a race only when it's necessary for the greatest good. And we would especially dislike having to dispose of the Damorlanti."

"What's wrong with them?" Clarey asked, pushing away his half-finished crème brulée a la Betelgeuse with a sigh. "Are they excessively belligerent, then?"

"No more belligerent than any intelligent life-form which has pulled itself up by its bootstraps."

"Rigid?" Clarey suggested. "Unadaptable? Intolerant? Indolent? Personally offensive?"

*

Spano smiled. He leaned back with half-shut eyes, as if this were a guessing game. "None of those."

"Then why consider disposing of them?" Clarey asked. "They sound pretty decent for natives. Don't wipe them out; even an ilf has a right to live."

"Clarey," the girl said, "you're drunk."

"I'm in full command of my faculties," he assured her. "My wits are all about me, moving me to ask how you could possibly expect to use a secret agent on Damorlan if there are no colonists. What would he disguise himself as—a touring Earth official?" He laughed with modest triumph.

Spano smiled. "He could disguise himself as one of them. They're humanoid."

"*That* humanoid?"

"That humanoid. So there you have the problem in a nutshell."

But Clarey still couldn't see that there was a problem. "I thought we—the human race, that is—were supposed to be the very apotheosis of life species."

"So we are. And that's the impression we've conveyed to such other intelligent life-forms as we've taken under our aegis. What we're afraid of is that the other ilfs might become . . . confused when they see the Damorlanti, think they're the ruling race." Leaning forward, he pounded so loudly on the table both the others jumped. "This is our galaxy and we don't intend that anyone, humanoid or otherwise, is going to forget it!"

"You're drunk, too, Steff," the girl said. She had changed completely; her coquetry had dropped as if it were another mask. And it had been, Clarey thought—an advertising mask. An offer had been made, and, if he accepted it, he would get probably not Han herself but a reasonable facsimile.

He tried to sort things out in his whizzing brain. "But why should the other ilfs ever see a Damorlant?" he asked, enunciating very precisely. "I've never seen another life-form to speak of. I thought the others weren't allowed off-planet—except the Baluts, and there's no mistaking them, is there?" For the Baluts, although charming, were unmistakably non-human, being purplish, amiable, and octopoid.

"We don't forbid the ilfs to go off-planet," Spano proclaimed. "That would be tyrannical. We simply don't allow them passage in our spaceships. Since they don't have any of their own, they can't leave."

SENTRY OF THE SKY

"Then you're afraid the Damorlanti will develop space travel on their own," Clarey cried. "Superior race—seeking after knowledge—spread their wings and soar to the stars." He flapped his arms and fell off the stool.

"Really, Steff," Han said, motioning for the servo-mechanism to pick Clarey up, "this is no way to conduct an interview."

"I am a creative artist," the general said thickly. "I believe in suiting the interview to the occasion. Clarey understands, for he, too, is an artist." The general sneezed and rubbed his nose with his silver sleeve. "Listen to me, boy. The Damorlanti are a fine, creative, productive race. It isn't generally known, but they developed the op fastener for evening wear, two of the new scents on the roster come from Damorlan, and the snettis is an adaptation of a Damorlant original. Would you want a species as artistic as that to be annihilated by an epidemic?"

"Do our germs work on them?" Clarey wanted to know.

"That hasn't been established yet. But their germs certainly work on us." The general sneezed again. "That's where I got this sinus trouble, last voyage to Damorlan. But you'll be inoculated, of course. Now we know what to watch out for, so you'll be perfectly safe. That is, as far as disease is concerned."

*

His face assumed a stern, noble aspect. "Naturally, if you're discovered as a spy, we'll have to repudiate you. You must know that from the tri-dis."

"But I haven't said I would go!" Clarey howled. "And I can't see why you'd want *me*, anyway!"

"Modest," the general said, lighting a smoke-stick. "An admirable trait in a young intelligence operative—or, indeed, anyone. Have a smoke-stick?"

14

Clarey hesitated. He had never tried one; he had always wanted to. "Don't, Clarey," the girl advised. "You'll be sick."

She spoke with authority and reason. Clarey shook his head.

The general inhaled and exhaled a cloud of smoke in the shape of a bunnit. "The Damorlanti look like us, but because they look like us, that doesn't mean they think like us. They may not have the least idea of developing space travel, simply be interested in developing thought, art, ideals, splendid cultural things like that. We don't know enough about them; we may be making mountains out of molehills."

"Martian molehills," Clarey snickered.

"Precisely," the general agreed. "Except that there are no moles on Mars either."

"But I still can't understand. Why *me?*"

The general leaned forward and said in a confidential tone, "We want to understand the true Damorlan. Our observations have been too superficial; couldn't help being. There we come, blasting out of the skies with the devil of a noise, running all over the planet as if we owned it. You know how those skyboys throw their gravity around."

Clarey nodded. *Sentries of the Sky* had kept him well informed on such matters.

"So what we want is a man who can go to Damorlan for five or ten years and become a Damorlant in everything but basic loyalties. A man who will absorb the very spirit of the culture, but in terms our machines can understand and interpret." Spano stood erect. "You, Clarey, are that man!"

The girl applauded. "Well done, Steff! You finally got it right side up!"

"But I've lived twenty-eight years on this planet and I'm not a part of its culture," Clarey protested. "I'm a lonely, friendless man—you must know that if you've deep-probed me—so why should I put up a front and be brave and proud about it?"

*

Then he gave a short, bitter laugh. "I see. That's the reason you want me. I have no roots, no ties; I belong nowhere. Nobody loves me. Who else, you think, but a man like me would spend ten years on an alien planet as an alien?"

"A patriot, Sub-Archivist," the general said sternly. "By God, sir, a patriot!"

"There's nothing I'd like better than to see Terra and all its colonies go up in smoke. Mind you," Clarey added quickly, for he was not as drunk as all that, "I've nothing against the government. It's a purely personal grievance."

The general unsteadily patted his arm. "You're detached, m'boy. You can examine an alien planet objectively, without trying to project your own cultural identity upon it, because you have no cultural identity."

"How about physical identity?" Clarey asked. "They can't be ex-exactly like us. Against the laws of nature."

"The laws of man are higher than the laws of nature," the general said, waving his arm. A gout of smoke curled around his head and became a halo. "Very slight matter of plastic surgery. And we'll change you back as soon as you return." Then he sat down heavily. "How many young men in your position get an opportunity like this? Permanent U-E status, a hundred thousand credits a year and, of course, on Damorlan you'd be on an expense account; our money's no good there. By the time you got back, there'd be about a million and a half waiting for you, with interest. You could buy all the instruments and tape all the music you wanted. And, if the Musicians' Guild puts up a fuss, you could buy it, too. Don't let anybody kid you about the wheel, son; money was mankind's first significant invention."

"But ten years. That's a long time away from home."

"Home is where the heart is, and you wanting to see your own planet go up in a puff of smoke—why, even an ilf wouldn't say a thing like that!" Spano shook his head. "That's too detached for me to understand. You'll find the years will pass quickly on Damorlan. You'll have stimulating work to do; every moment will be a challenge. When it's all over, you'll be only thirty-eight—the very prime of life. You won't have aged even that much, because you'll be entitled to longevity treatments at regular intervals.

"So think it over, m'boy." He rose waveringly and clapped Clarey on the shoulder. "And take the rest of the afternoon off; I'll fix it with Archives. We wouldn't want you coming back from Classification intoxicated." He winked. "Make a very bad impression on your co-workers."

Han masked herself and escorted Clarey to the restaurant portway. "Don't believe everything he says. But I think you'd better accept the offer."

"I don't have to," Clarey said.

"No," she agreed, "you don't. But you'd better."

*

Clarey took the cheap underground route home. His antiseptic little two-room apartment seemed even bleaker than usual. He dialed a dyspep pill from the auto-spensor; the lunch was beginning to tell on him. And that evening he couldn't even take an interest in *Sentries of the Sky*, which, though he'd never have admitted it, was his favorite program. He had no friends; nobody would miss him if he left Earth or died or anything. The general's right, he thought; I might as well be an alien on an alien planet. At least I'll be paid better. And he wondered whether, in lighter gravity, his spirits might not get a lift.

He dragged himself to work the next day. He found someone did care after all. "Well, Sub-Archivist Clarey," Chief Section Archivist MacFingal snarled, "I would have expected to see more sparkle in your eye, more pep in your step, after a whole day of nothing but sweet rest."

"But—but General Spano said it would be all right if I didn't report back in the afternoon."

"Oh, it is all right, Sub-Archivist, no question of that. How could I dare to complain about a man who has such powerful friends? I suppose if I gave you the Sagittarius files to reorganize, you'd go running to your friend General Spano, sniveling about cruel and unfair treatment."

So Clarey started reorganizing the Sagittarius files—a sickeningly dull task which should by rights have gone to a junior archivist. All morning he couldn't help thinking about Damorlan—its invigorating atmosphere, its pleasant climate, its presumed absence of archives and archivists. During his lunchstop he looked up the planet in the files. There was only a small part of a tape on it. There might be more in the Classified Files. It was, of course, forbidden to view secretapes without a direct order from the Chief Archivist, but the tapes were locked by the same code as the rare editions. After all, he told himself, I have a legitimate need for the information.

So he punched for Damorlan in the secret files. He put the tape in the viewer. He saw the natives. Cold shock filled him, and then hot fury. They were humanoid all right—pallid, pale-haired creatures. Objective viewpoint, he thought furiously; detachment be damned! I was picked *because I look like one of them!*

18

He was wrenched away from the viewer. "Sub-Archivist Clarey, what is the meaning of this?" Chief Section Archivist MacFingal demanded. "You know what taking a secretape out without permission means?"

Clarey knew. The reorientation machine. "Ask General Spano," he said in a constricted voice. "He'll tell you it's all right."

*

General Spano said that it was, indeed, all right. "I'm so glad to hear you've decided to join us. Splendid career for an enterprising young man. Smoke-stick?"

Clarey refused; he no longer had any interest in trying one.

"Don't look so grim," Spano said jovially. "You'll like the Damorlanti once you get to know them. Very affectionate people. Haven't had any major wars for several generations. Currently there are just a few skirmishes at the poles and you ought to be able to keep away from those easily. And they'll simply love you."

"But I don't like anyone," Clarey said. "And I don't see why the Damorlanti should like me," he added fairly.

"I'll tell you why! Because it'll be your job to *make* them like you. You've got to be friendly and outgoing if it kills you. Anyone can develop a winning personality if he sets his mind to it. I though you said you watched the tri-dis!"

"I—I don't always watch the commercials," Clarey admitted.

"Oh, well, we all have our little failings." Spano leaned forward, his voice now pitched to persuasive decibels. "Normally, of course, you wouldn't stoop to hypocrisy to gain friends, and quite right, too—people should accept you as you are or they wouldn't be worthy of becoming your friends. But this is different. You have to be what they want, because you want something from them. You'll have to suffer rebuffs and humiliations and never show resentment."

"In other words," Clarey said, "a secret agent is supposed to forget all about such concepts as self-respect."

"If necessary, yes. But here self-respect doesn't enter into it. These aren't people and they don't really matter. You wouldn't be humiliated, would you, if you tried to pat a dog and it snarled at you?"

"Steff, he's got to think of them as people until he's definitely given them a clean bill of health," Han Vollard protested. "Otherwise, the whole thing won't work."

"Well," the general temporized, "think of them as people, then, but as inferior people. Let them snoop and pry and sneer. Always, at the back of your mind, you'll have the knowledge that this is all a sham, that someday they'll get whatever it is they deserve. You might even think of it as a game, Clarey—no more personal than when you fail to get the gardip ball into the loop."

"I don't happen to play gardip, General," Clarey reminded him coldly. Gardip was strictly a U-E pastime. And, in any case, Clarey was not a gamesman.

He was put through intensive indoctrination, given accelerated courses in the total secret agent curriculum: Self-Defense and Electronics, Decoding and Resourcefulness, Xenopsychology and Acting.

"There are eight cardinal rules of acting," the robocoach told him. "The first is: Never Identify. You'll never be able to become the character you're playing, because you aren't that character—the playwright gave birth to him, not your mother. Therefore—"

"But I'm only going to play one role," Clarey broke in. "All I need to know is how to play that role well and convincingly. My life may depend on it."

"I teach acting," the robocoach said loftily. "I don't run a charm school. If you come to me, you learn—or, at least, are exposed to—all I have to offer. I refuse to tailor my art to any occasional need. Now, the second cardinal rule. . . . "

*

Clarey was glad he could absorb the languages and social structure of the planet through the impersonal hypno-tapes. He had to learn more than one language because the planet was divided into several national units, each speaking a different tongue. Inefficient as far as planetary operation went, but advantageous to him, Han Vollard pointed out, because, though he'd work in Vangtor, he would be supposed to have originated in Ventimor; hence his accent.

"Work?" Clarey asked. "I thought I was going to be an undercover agent."

"You'll have a cover job," she explained wearily. "You can't just wander around with no visible source of income, unless you're a member of the nobility, and it would be risky to elevate you to the peerage."

"What kind of a job will I have?" Clarey asked, brightening a little at the idea of possibly having something interesting to do.

"They call it *librarian*. I'm not exactly sure what it is, but Colonel Blynn—he's our chief officer on the planet—says that after indoctrination you ought to be able to handle it."

Clarey already knew that jobs on Damorlan weren't officially assigned, but that employer and employee somehow managed to find each other and work out arrangements themselves. Sometimes, Han now explained, employers would advertise for employees. Colonel Blynn had answered such a job in Vangtor on his behalf from an accommodation address in Ventimor. "You were hired sight unseen, because you came cheap. So they probably won't check your references. Let's hope not, anyway."

*

The trip to Damorlan was one long aching agony. Since luxury liners naturally didn't touch on Damorlan, he was sent out on a service freighter, built for maximum stowage rather than comfort. Most of the time he was spacesick. The only thing that comforted him was that it would be ten years before he'd have to go back.

They landed on the Earthmen's spaceport—the only spaceport, of course—at Barshwat, and he was hustled off to Earth Headquarters in an animal-drawn cart that made him realize there were other ailments besides spacesickness.

"Afraid you're going to have to hole up in my suite while you're with us," Colonel Blynn apologized when Clarey was safely inside. "The rest of the establishment is crawling with native servants—daytimes, anyway; they sleep out—but they have orders never to come near my quarters."

He looked interestedly at Clarey. "Amazing how the plastosurgeons got you to look exactly like a native. Those boys really know their stuff. Maybe I *will* have my nose fixed next time I go Earthside."

Clarey glared venomously at the tall, handsome, dark young officer.

"Don't worry," Blynn soothed him. "I'm sure when you go back they'll be able to make you look exactly the way you were before."

He gave Clarey a general briefing and explained to him that the additional allowance he'd be receiving—since he couldn't be expected to live on a Damorlant salary—would come from an alleged rich aunt in Barshwat.

"Where'll you get the native currency?" Clarey asked.

"We do some restricted trading with the natives, bring materials that're in short supply; salt, breakfast cereals, pigments, thread—stuff like that. Nothing strategic, nothing they could possibly use against us . . . unless they decide to strangle us with our own string." He guffawed ear-splittingly.

*

One rainy evening a couple of Earth officers hustled Clarey into a hax-cart. A little later, equipped with a native kit, an itinerary, and a ticket purchased in Ventimor, he was left a short distance from a large track-car station.

He was so numb with fright he had to force himself to move in the right direction leg by leg. He gained a little confidence when he was able to find the terminus without needing to ask directions; he even managed to find the right chain of cars and a place to sit in one of them. He didn't realize that this was something of an achievement until he discovered that certain later arrivals had to stand. He wondered why more tickets were issued than there were seats available, then realized the answer was simple—primitives couldn't count very accurately.

Creakily and slowly, the chain got under way. Clarey's terror mounted. Here he was, wearing strange clothes, on a strange world, surrounded by strange creatures. They aren't really repulsive, he told himself; they look like people; they look like me.

Some of the natives seemed to be staring at him. His heart began to beat loudly. Could they hear it? Did their hearts beat the same way? Was their hearing more acute than his? The tapes had seemed so full of information; now he saw how full of holes they'd been. Then he noticed that the natives were staring at each other. His heart quieted. Only a local custom. After a while, little conversational groups formed. No one spoke to him, for he spoke to no one. He was not yet ready to thrust himself upon them; he had enough to do to reach his destination successfully.

SENTRY OF THE SKY

He tried to follow the conversations for practice and to keep his mind off his fears. The male next to him was talking to the male opposite about the weather and its effect on the sirtles. The three females on his other side were telling each other how their respective offspring were doing in school. Some voices he couldn't identify with owners were complaining how much sagor and titulwirt cost these days. I don't know why the government is so worried, he thought; they're not really very human at all.

The chain had been scheduled to reach the end of its run in three hours. It took closer to five. He got off at what would have been around midnight on Earth, and the terminus where he was supposed to take the next chain was almost empty of people, completely empty of cars. Although it was still a few minutes before his car was due, he was worried. Finally, he approached a native.

"Is this—is this not where the 39:12 to Zrig is destined to appear?" he asked, conscious as he uttered Vangtort aloud for the first time that his phrasing was not entirely colloquial.

The native stared at him with small pale eyes and bit his middle finger. "Stranger, eh?" he asked in a small pale voice.

"Yes." The native waited. "I come from Ventimor," Clarey told him. Nosy native, he thought furiously; prying primitive.

"You don't hafta shout," the native said. "I'm not deef."

Clarey realized what he hadn't noted consciously before—the natives spoke much more softly than Earthmen. Local custom two.

"You'll be finding things a lot different here in Vangtor," the native told him. "Livelier, more up to date. F'rinstance, do the cars always run on time in Ventimor?"

"Yes," Clarey said firmly.

24

"Well, they don't here. Know why? That's because we've got more'n one chain of 'em." He made a noise like a wounded turshi. He was laughing.

*

Clarey smiled until his gums ached. "About the 39:12? It is rather important to me, as I understand the next chain does not leave for several days."

The native lifted a chronometer hanging around his neck. "Ought to get in around 40 or so," he said. "Whyn't you get yourself a female or a bite to eat?" He waved his hand toward the two trade booths that were still open for business.

Clarey was very hungry. But, as he got near the food booth, the stench and the sight of the utensils were too much for him. He went back to the carways and sat huddled on a banquette until his chain came in at 40:91.

The car he picked was empty, so he stretched out on the seat and slept until it got to Zrig, very early in the morning. When he got out, day was dawning and a food booth hadn't had time to accumulate odors so he climbed to one of the perches and pointed to something that looked like a lopsided pie and something else that looked like coffee. Neither was what it appeared to be, but the pseudo-pie was edible and the pseudo-coffee was good. Somehow, the food seemed to diminish his fright; it made the world less strange.

"Where you going, stranger?" the native asked, resting his arms on the top of the booth.

"Katund," Clarey said. The other looked puzzled. "It is a village near Zrig."

"That a fact?" The native bit his little finger. "You look like a city feller to me."

"That is correct," Clarey said patiently. "I come from Qytet. It is a place of some size." He waited a decent interval before collapsing his smile.

"Now, why would a smart-looking young fellow like you want to go to a place like this Katund, eh?"

Clarey started to shrug, then remembered that was not a Damorlant gesture. "I have received employment there."

"I should think you'd be able to do better'n that." The native nibbled at his thumb. "What did you say you worked at?"

"I didn't. I am a librarian."

The native turned away and began to rinse his utensils. "In that case, I guess Katund's as good a place as any."

Surely, Clarey thought, even a Damorlant would at this point rise up and smite the food merchant with one of his own platters. Then he forgot his anger in apprehension. What in the name of whatever gods they worshipped on this planet could a librarian possibly be?

He got up and was about to go. Then he remembered to be friendly and outgoing. "I have never tasted better food," he told the native. "Not even in Barshwat."

The native picked up the coin Clarey had left by way of tip and bit it. Apparently it passed the test. "Stop here next time you're passing this way," he advised, "and I'll really serve you something to write home about!"

*

The omnibus for Katund proved to be nothing but a large cart drawn by a team of hax. Clarey waited for internal manifestations as he rode. None came. I've found my land legs, he thought, or, rather, my land stomach. And with the hax jogging along the quiet lanes of Vangtor, he found himself almost at peace.

Earth was completely urbanized: there were the great metropolises; there were the parks; there were the oceans. That was all. So to him the Vangtort countryside looked like a huge park, with grass and trees and flowers that were slightly unrealistic in color, but beautiful just the same—even more, perhaps. It was idyllic. There's bound to be some catch, he thought.

The other passengers, who'd been talking together in low tones, turned toward Clarey. "You'll be the new librarian, I take it?" the tallest observed. He was a bulky creature, wearing a rich but sober cloak that came down to his ankles.

For a moment Clarey couldn't understand him; the local dialect seemed to thicken the words. "Why, yes. How did you know that?"

The native wiggled his ears. "Not many folks come to Katund and a new librarian's expected, so it wasn't hard to figure. Except you don't look my idea of a librarian."

Clarey nervously smoothed the dark red cloak that covered him from shoulder to mid-calf. Was it too loud? Too quiet? Too short?

"What give you the idea of comin' to Katund?" the oldest and smallest of the three asked in a whistling voice. "It's no place anybody who wasn't born here'd choose."

"Most young fellers favor the city," the third—a barrel-shaped individual—agreed. "I'd of gone there myself when I was a lad, if Dad hadn't needed somebody to take over the Purple Furbush when he was gone."

"Maybe he's runnin' away," the ancient sibilated. "When I was a boy, there was a feller from the city came here; turned out to be a thief." All three stared at Clarey.

"I—I replied to an advertisement in the Dordonec District Bulletin," he said carefully. "I wished for a position that was peaceful and quiet. I am recovering from an overset of the nervous system."

The oldest one said, "That'd account for it right enough."

Clarey gritted his teeth and beamed at them.

"Typical idiot smile," the ancient whispered. "Noticed it myself right off, but I didn't like to say."

"Is it right to have a librarian that isn't all there?" the proprietor of the Furbush asked. "Foreigner, too. I mean to say—the young ones use him more'n most."

"We've got to take what we can get," the biggest native said. "Katund's funds are running mighty low."

"What can you expect when you ballot yourself a salary raise every year?" the old one whistled. The other two made animal noises. Clarey must not jump; he must learn to laugh like a turshi if he hoped to be the life of any Damorlant party.

*

The big one stood up as well as he could in the swaying cart. "Guess I'd better introduce myself," he said, holding out a sturdily shod foot. "I'm Malesor, headman of Katund. This is Piq; he deals in blots and snarls. And Hanxi here's the inn-keeper."

"My name is Balt," Clarey said. "I am honored by this meeting." And he went through the conventional toe-touching with each one.

"Guess you'll be putting up with me until you've found permanent quarters, Til Balt," Hanxi said. "Not that you could do much better than make your permanent home at the Purple Furbush. You'll find life more comfortable than if you lodge with a private fam'ly. Bein' a young unmarried man—" he twisted his nose suggestively—"you'd naturally want a bit of freedom, excitement."

"Remember he's a librarian," Piq whistled. "He might not appreciate as good a time as most young fellers."

Clarey was glad when a cluster of domes appearing over the horizon indicated that they'd reached Katund. He looked about him curiously. The countryside he'd been able to equate with a park, but this small aggregate of detached dwellings bore no relationship to anything in his experience.

His kit was dexterously removed from his hand. "Guess you'll want to check in first," Hanxi said, "so I'll just take your gear over to the inn for you."

He pointed out a small dome shading from lavender at the bottom to rose pink on top. Over the door were glittering symbols which Clarey was able to decipher after a moment's concentration as "Dordonec District Public Library—Katund Branch," and underneath, in smaller letters, "Please Blow Nose Before Entering."

Hesitantly, he touched the screen that covered the portway. It rolled back. He went inside.

At his first sight of what filled the shelves from floor to topmost curve of the dome, Clarey became charged with fury. The ancient books in the glass cases back on Earth were of a different shape and substance, but, "My God," he cried aloud, "it's nothing but another archive!"

The female in charge glared at him. "Silence, please!"

Suddenly the anger left him, and the fear. He was no longer a stranger on a strange world. He was an archivist in an archive.

She took a better look at him and the local equivalent of a bright smile shone on her face. "May I help you, til?" she asked in a softer, sweeter voice.

"I am Balt, til," he said. "I am the new librarian."

She came out from behind the desk to offer the ceremonial toe touch. "I'm Embelsira, the head librarian, and I am very glad to see you!" Her tone was warm; she really seemed to mean it. "Everything's in such a mess," she went on. "I've needed help so very badly, so very long." She looked up at him, for she was a good deal shorter than he. "So glad," she murmured, "so very, very glad to see you, really."

"Well, now you have help," he said with quiet strength. "Where are the files?"

They were written instead of punched, of alien design, in an alien language, arranged according to alien patterns, but he understood them at a glance. "These will need to be re-organized from top to bottom," he said.

"Yes, Til Balt," she said demurely. "Whatever you say."

*

Once every six months, Clarey went for a long weekend to visit his "Aunt Askidush" in Barshwat. Barshwat was the largest city on Damorlan; it was the capital of Vintnor—the greatest nation. Earthmen, Clarey thought, as he traveled there in the comparative luxury of a first-class compartment—as a rich nephew, he saw no real reason to travel third-class—were disgustingly obvious.

That first time, he was five hours late, and Blynn was a nervous wreck. "I was afraid you'd been killed or discovered or God knows," he babbled, practically embracing Clarey in a fervency of relief. "I was afraid—"

"Come, come, Colonel," Clarey interrupted, striding past him, "you know how inefficient Damorlant transport is, and I had to make two chain connections."

"Of course," the colonel said, wiping the perspiration off his forehead. "Of course. And you must be dead tired. Sit down; let me take your cloak—"

"How about the servants?" Clarey asked.

"This is their weekend off." Blynn pulled himself together. "Really, my dear fellow, I've been in this business longer than you. I know what precautions to take."

"Never can be too careful."

"I see you've got yourself another cloak," the colonel said as he hung it in the guest snap. "Very handsome. I've never seen one like it."

"Yes. As a matter of fact, several people on the chains wanted to know where I'd got it."

"Where *did* you get it?" asked Blynn, feeling the material. "Might go well as an export."

"Afraid it couldn't be exported. It's a custom job, you see. Hand-woven, hand-decorated. It was a birthday present."

The colonel stared at him.

"Well," Clarey said, "if you didn't expect me to get birthday presents, you shouldn't have put a birth date on my identity papers. My boss baked me a melxhane—"

"Your boss!"

"The relationship between employer and employee is much different from the way it is on Earth," Clarey explained. Reaching over, he flipped the switch on the recorder and repeated the statement, adding, "Embelsira is kind, considerate, helpful; she can't do enough for me." He put his mouth close to the mechanism. "Be sure to tell MacFingal that."

"Now, now," the colonel said, turning the switch off. He pushed a small tea wagon over to Clarey. "You must be starving. Have some sandwiches and coffee. I'm sure you'll be glad to taste good Earth food again."

"Yes, indeed," Clarey said, trying not to make a face. "Er—shouldn't we start recording while everything's fresh in my mind?"

"Might as well," the colonel said, flipping the switch again. "Pity we don't have a probe here. Would save so much time. But, of course, it's an expensive installation. All right, Clarey, over to you."

SENTRY OF THE SKY

*

Clarey choked on a mouthful of sandwich and hesitated. "Begin with your very first impressions," the colonel urged.

"Well, the archives—the library—was in a real mess. Took me over two weeks to get it in even roughly decent shape. Three different systems of classification and, added to that—"

"Not so much the library, old chap. Leave the technical stuff for later. What I meant was your first impressions of the natives. . . . Is something wrong with the coffee? And you've hardly touched your sandwich. Maybe you'd like another kind. I have several varieties here—ham and cheese and—"

"Oh, no," Clarey protested. "The one I have is fine. It's just that I'm—well, to tell you the truth," he confessed, "I've grown accustomed to Damorlant food."

"Don't see how you could," the colonel said. "Nauseating stuff—to my way of thinking," he added politely. He opened a sandwich and inspected the filling.

"You've only eaten at public places. Even the better restaurants don't put themselves out for Earthmen, say they have no—palates, I guess the word would be. But you ought to taste my landlady's cooking!"

"All this is being taped, you know. They'll have to listen to every word on Earth."

"If only I could convey the true picture through words. Her ragouts are rhapsodies, her soufflés symphonies—I'm using rough Terrestrial equivalents, of course—"

"The cuisine comes later, please. Over-all impressions first."

"Well," Clarey began again, "at first I was a bit surprised that you'd stuck me in a quarter-credit place like Katund. Naturally in a village the people'd be more backward than in the cities, so you'd have a poorer idea of how they were developing. Then I realized that you couldn't help putting me there, that you probably couldn't write a letter good enough to get me a job in any of the big centers. Embelsira said she was surprised to find me so much more literate than she would have expected from the letter."

The colonel sat erect huffily. "I've never pretended to be a philologist. And, anyway, Damorlan isn't like Earth. Here the heartbeat of the planet is in its villages."

"Earth hasn't any villages, so the comparison doesn't apply." Clarey cleared his throat. "Don't you have anything to drink except coffee?"

"Tea?"

"That would be better. Do you know the Katundi have a special variety of tea, or something very like it, which is—"

"Tell me what they think of Earthmen," the colonel interrupted desperately.

"Not much. What I mean is, nobody in Katund's actually had any contact with them, though they've heard of them, of course. Every now and then there's a little article in the Dordonec Bulletin from their Barshwat correspondent, and sometimes, if there isn't any real news, he gives a couple of inches to the Earthmen."

"Exactly how do they regard us?" the colonel asked as he spooned tea into the pot. "Demi-gods? Superior beings? Are they in great awe of us?"

"They regard us as visitors from another planet," Clarey said. "They don't realize from quite how far away we hail, think it's only a matter of a solar system or two, but they've got the general idea. Don't forget, they may not be a mechanical people, but they do have some idea of astronomy. They're not illiterate clods."

"What do they think of our spaceships? Great silver birds, something like that?"

SENTRY OF THE SKY

*

Sighing deeply, Clarey said, "They think our spaceships are cars that fly through the sky without tracks. And they think it's silly, our having machines to fly in the sky and none to go on the ground. There's an old Dordonec proverb: 'One must run before one must fly.' Originally applied to birds, but—"

"But what else do they think about us?"

Clarey was hurt. "That's what I was getting to, if you'll only give me time. After all, I've been speaking Vangtort for six months and it's a little hard to go back to Terran and organize my thoughts at the same time."

"Terribly sorry," the colonel apologized, handing him a cup of tea. "Carry on."

"Thank you. They say if you—if we—are so smart, why do we use hax or the chains like anybody else? They think somebody else must have given us the starships, or else we stole them. That's mostly Piq's idea; he's the village lawyer and, of course, lawyers are apt to think in terms like that."

"Um," the colonel said. "We didn't think it would be a good idea to introduce ground cars. Upset their traffic and cause dissatisfied yearnings."

"They're satisfied with their hax carts. They're not in any hurry to get anywhere. But Katund's a village. Attitudes may be different in the cities."

"You stick with your village, old chap. If you feel a wild urge for city life, you can always take a weekend trip to Zrig. Stay at the Zrig Grasht; it's the only decent inn. By the way, you spoke of a landlady. Do you mean at the inn?"

No, Clarey told him, at first he had put up at the inn, but he found the place noisy, the cooking poor, and the pallet covers dirty. Besides,

Hanxi had kept importuning him to go on visits to a nearby township where he promised him a good time.

"I was wondering, though," Clarey finished, "if it would be possible for an Earthman and a Damorlant to—er—have a good time together."

"Been wondering myself!" the colonel said eagerly. "I didn't dare ask on my own behalf, but it's your job, isn't it? I'll check back with the X-T boys on Earth. Go on with your story."

*

As a resident of the inn, Clarey told Colonel Blynn, he'd found that he was expected to join the men in the bar parlor every evening, where they'd drink and exchange appropriate stories. But he'd choked on the squfur and was insufficiently familiar with the local mores to be able to appreciate the stories, let alone tell any. He'd concentrated on smiling and agreeing with whatever anybody said, with the result that the others began to agree with Piq that he was a bit cracked. "They were, for the most part, polite enough to me, but I could sense the gulf. I was a stranger, a city man, and probably a bit of a lunatic."

A few of the younger ones hadn't even been polite. "They used to insult me obliquely," Clarey went on, "and whisper things I only half-heard. I pretended I didn't hear at all. I stood them drinks and told them what a lovely place Katund was, so much cleaner and prettier and friendlier than the city. That just seemed to confirm their impression that I was an idiot."

He stopped, took a sip of tea, and continued, "The females were friendly enough, though. Every time they came into the library they'd always stop for a chat. And they were very hospitable—invited me to outdoor luncheons, temple gatherings, things like that. Embelsira—she's the chief librarian—got quite annoyed because she said they made so much noise when they all gathered round my desk."

He paused and blushed. "I have an idea that—well, the ladies don't find me unattractive. I mean they're not really ladies. That is, they're perfect ladies; they're just not women."

"I'm not a bit surprised," the colonel nodded sagely. "Very well-set-up young fellow for a native—only natural they should take a liking to you. And only natural the men shouldn't."

Clarey gave an embarrassed grin. "One evening I was sitting in the bar-parlor, talking to Kuqal and Gazmor, two of the older men. And then Mundes came in; he's the town muscle boy. You know the type—one in every tri-di series. He was rather unpleasant. I pretended to think he was joking. I've learned to laugh like one of them. Listen." He gave a creditable imitation of an agonized turshi.

*

The colonel shuddered. "I'm sure if anything would convince the chaps back on Earth that the Damorlanti aren't human, that would do it. What then?"

"Finally he made a remark impugning the virility of librarians that I simply could not ignore, so I emptied my mug of squfur in his face."

"Stout fellow!"

"I knew he'd attack me and probably beat me up, but I thought that perhaps if I put up a show of courage they'd respect me. There was something like that in *Sentries of the Sky* a year or so ago—but of course you'd have missed that episode; you were up here. Anyhow, as I expected, he hit me. And then I hit him. . . . " He smiled reminiscently into his cup of tea.

"And then?"

"I beat him," Clarey said simply. "I still can't figure out how I did it. I think it must be because my muscles are heavier-gravity type." He smiled again. "And I beat him good. He couldn't dance at the temple for weeks."

The colonel's jaw dropped. "He's a temple dancer?"

"Chief temple dancer. I was a little worried about that, because I didn't want to get in bad theologically. So I went to the priest and apologized for any inconvenience I might have caused. He said not to worry; Mundes had had it coming to him for a long time and his one regret was that he hadn't been there to see it. Then we touched toes and he said he liked to see a young fellow with brawn who also took an interest in cultural pursuits like reading. He trusted I'd have a beneficial effect on the youth of the village. And then he asked me to fill in for Mundes as chief temple dancer until he—ah—recovered. It's a great honor, you know!" he said sharply, as the colonel seemed more moved to mirth than awe. "But I've never been much of a dancing man and that's what I told him."

"Very well done," the colonel said approvingly. "But you still haven't explained where you got lodgings and a landlady."

"She's Embelsira's mother. I was invited over for dinner from time to time. . . . It's a local custom," he explained as Blynn's eyebrows went up. "So, when Embelsira told me her mother happened to have a compartment to let with meals included, I jumped at it. Blynn, you really ought to taste those pastries of hers!"

The colonel managed to divert him onto some of the other aspects of Katundut life. When he'd finished taping everything he had to say, the colonel gave him a list of artifacts and small-sized flora and fauna the specialists on Earth wanted him to collect for his next trip, providing he could do so without arousing attention or violating tabus.

SENTRY OF THE SKY

They shook hands. "Clarey," the colonel said, "you've done splendidly. Earth will be proud of you. And you might bring along one or two of those pastries, by the way."

*

When Clarey got back to Katund, Embelsira and her mother gave a little welcome home party for him. "Nothing elaborate," the widow said. "Just a few neighbors and friends, some simple refreshments."

The tiny residential dome was packed with people; the refreshments, Clarey thought, as he munched industriously, were magnificent. But then he'd been forced to live on Earth food for a weekend, so he was no judge.

After they'd finished eating, the young people folded the furniture, and, while one of the boys played upon a curious instrument that was string and percussion and brass all at once, the others danced.

Clarey made no attempt to participate. In his early youth, he'd flopped at the Earth hops—and the Damorlanti had a distinctly more Dionysian culture than his home world. He stood and watched them leaping and twirling. When they'd dropped, temporarily exhausted, he made his way over to the musician, whom he recognized as one of Piq's numerous grandsons; this one was Rini, he thought.

"Is that difficult to learn?" he asked, touching the instrument.

"The ulerin is extremely difficult," the boy said importantly. "It takes years and years of practice. And you've got to have the touch to begin with. Not many do. All our family have the touch, my brother Irik most of all. He's in Barshwat, studying to be a famous musician."

Clarey looked at the ulerin with unmistakable wistfulness.

"Care to try it?" the boy asked. "But, mind, you have to pay for any bladders you burst."

"I shall be very careful," Clarey said, taking the instrument reverently in his hands. He had never touched a musical instrument before—an Earth instrument would have been no less unfamiliar, no more wonderful. Gently he began to pluck and bang and blow, in imitation of the way the boy had done, and, though the sounds that came out didn't have the same smoothness, still they didn't fall harshly on his ears. The others stopped talking and listened; it would have been difficult for them to do otherwise, as he was unable to find the muting device.

"Sounds like the death wail of a hix," Piq sibilated, but he added grudgingly, "Foreigner or not, I have to say this for him—he's got the touch."

"Yes, he's got the touch," others agreed. "You always can tell."

Rini smiled at Clarey. "I believe you do. I'll teach you to play, if you like."

"I would, very much." Clarey was about to offer to pay for the lessons; then he remembered that, though this would have been the right thing on Earth, it would be wrong on Damorlan. "If it is not too much trouble," he finished.

"It's the kind of trouble I like." The boy twisted his nose at Clarey. "Sometime you can hide the reserved books for me."

*

After the guests had gone, Clarey insisted on helping the women with the putting away. "Well, as long as Embelsira has a pair of brawny arms to help her," the widow yawned, "I might as well be getting along to my pallet. I seem to get more and more tired these days—old age, I expect. One day I'll be so tired I'll never wake up and Embelsira'll be alone and what'll she do, poor thing? Who can live on a librarian's salary? Now, on two librarians' salaries—"

"Mother," Embelsira interrupted furiously, "you go to bed!"

She did, hurriedly.

"Don't worry, Embelsira," Clarey said. "She will be weaving away for decades yet. Everybody says she's the best weaver in the district," he added, to change the subject.

"Yes," Embelsira said as they gathered all the oddments the guests had left, "she's been offered a lot of money to go work in Zrig. But she won't leave Katund; she was born here, and so were her parents."

"I do not blame her for wanting to stay," he said. "It's a very—homelike place."

She sighed. "To us it is, but I don't suppose someone who's city born and bred would feel the same way. I know you won't let yourself stay buried here forever, and what will I—what will Mother and I ever do without you?"

"It is—very kind of you to say so," he replied. "I am honored."

The girl—she was still young enough to be called a girl, though no longer in her first youth—looked up at him. Blue eyes could be pleasing in their way. "Why are you always so stiff, so cold?"

"I am not cold," he said honestly. "I am—afraid."

"There is nothing to be afraid of. You're safe, among friends, no matter what you may have done back where you came from."

"But I have done nothing back there," he said. "Nothing at all. Perhaps that is the trouble with me."

She looked up at him and then away. "Then isn't it about time you started to do something?"

*

The next time he went to Barshwat he took a lot of luggage with him, because, besides the artifacts and the flora and fauna, he brought cold pastries for the colonel. The colonel ate one in silence, then said, "Try to get the recipe."

"By the way," said Clarey, "the X-T boys made a few mistakes. The bugg isn't an insect; it's a bird. And the lule isn't a bird; it's a flower. And the paparun isn't a flower; it's an insect."

"Oh, well, I guess they'll be able to straighten that out," the colonel said, licking crumbs from his thick fingers. "We do our jobs and they do theirs." He reached for another pastry.

"Take good care of the bugg," Clarey said. "He likes his morning seed mixed with milk; his evening seed with wine. His name is Mirti. He's very tame and affectionate. I—said I was bringing him to my aunt. . . . " He paused. "You *are* going to take him back alive, aren't you? You'd get so much more information that way."

"Wouldn't dream of hurting a hair—a feather—no, it is a hair, isn't it?—of the little fellow's head."

Clarey looked out of the window at the purple night sky. Then he turned back to the colonel. "I've been taking music lessons," he said defiantly.

"Fine! Every man should have a hobby!"

"But I've no music license."

"Come now, Clarey. You still don't seem to realize you're on Damorlan, not Earth. Not a blooded intelligence man yet! There aren't any guilds on Damorlan, so enjoy yourself."

"Speaking of that, did you find out about—er—Earthmen and—"

"Yes, I'd meant to drop you a note, but it seemed rather odd information for your aunt to be giving you. It's absolutely all right, old chap. Go ahead, have your bit of fun."

Clarey was unreasonably annoyed. "I wasn't thinking of what you're thinking. I mean—well, Katund is a village and the native morality is very strict in these matters."

"Afraid I don't quite follow you."

Clarey bit his finger. "Well," he finally admitted, "the truth of the matter is I'd like to get married."

The colonel was extremely surprised. "A legal arrangement! Is it absolutely necessary? How about the females that the innkeeper's so anxious to have you—ah—meet?"

*

Clarey didn't know how to explain. "Their standards of cleanliness. . . . " he began, and stopped. Then he started again: "I suppose I'd like a permanent companion."

"I don't suppose there's any real reason why you shouldn't enter into a legal liaison while you're here," said the colonel. "After all, it isn't as if the two races could interbreed. That could be decidedly awkward. Who's the lucky little lady?"

"My landlady's daughter," Clarey said.

"Your boss, eh? Flying high, aren't you, old chap?" His massive hand descended on Clarey's shoulder. Then he grew serious. "Can she cook like her mother?"

"Even better."

"My boy," the colonel said solemnly, "you have my unqualified blessing. And when I ask you to save me a piece of the wedding cake, I ask from the heart."

So, when Clarey went back to Katund, he asked Embelsira to marry him and she accepted. The whole village turned out for the wedding. Clarey managed to take some vocpix of the ceremonies for the X-Ts with a finger unit. I ought to get a handsome wedding present for this, he thought.

And, to his surprise, on the wedding day, an elaborate jewel-studded toilet service did arrive from Barshwat—with the affectionate regards of his aunt, who was too ill to travel. They tie up everything, he thought, but he knew it was a little more than simply remembering to pick up a loose end. The toilet set was vulgar, ostentatious, hideous—obviously selected with loving care and Terrestrial taste.

Everybody in Katund and a lot of people from the surrounding country came to look at it. It seemed to establish his eligibility beyond a doubt. "Never thought 'Belsira'd do it, and at her age, too," Piq was heard to comment. "But it looks like she really got herself a catch. What's a little weakness in the dome-top when there's money, too?"

*

The first three years of Clarey's marriage were happy ones. He and Embelsira got on very nicely together and, since he was fond of her mother, he didn't mind her constant presence too much. Once a week he took a ulerin lesson from Rini. He practiced assiduously and made progress that he himself could see was sensational. He did wish that Rini would accept money; it would have been so much less of a nuisance than replacing the music books the boy stole from the library, but he couldn't expect local customs to coincide with his own. The money, of course, didn't matter; he still wasn't living up to his allowance, although he was beginning to spread himself on elaborate custom-made cloaks and tunics. On Earth he had dressed soberly, according to his status, but here he felt entitled to cut a dash.

At the colonel's request, on his next trip to Barshwat he brought his ulerin and taped some native melodies. "I like 'em," the colonel said, nodding his head emphatically. "Catchy, very catchy. Hope the X-Ts appreciate them; they don't usually like music if it sounds at all human." And, catching the look on Clarey's face, "Well, you know what I mean. To them, if a tune can be hummed, it isn't authentic."

News of Clarey's skill on the ulerin spread through the countryside. When he played in the temple concerts, people sometimes came from as far away as Zrig to hear him. Clarey was a little disturbed about this, because he didn't subscribe to the local faith. But the high priest said, "My son, music knows no religious boundaries. Besides, when you play, we always get three times as much in the collection nets."

At the time Clarey got word from Barshwat that General Spano and the staff ship were expected shortly, he had risen to the post of chief librarian. Embelsira had retired to keep dome and wait for the young ones who would, of course, never come. Clarey had hired a hixhead of an assistant from Zrig to assist him; he saw now why the village had originally been grateful to get even a foreigner of doubtful background for the job.

"I'm going to have to stay at least a week with Aunt Askush this time," he told his wife. "Legal matters. I think she's drawing up a will or some such," he added, hoping that this would keep Embelsira happy and convinced.

Maybe it worked too well. "But why can't I come with you? I've always wanted so much to meet her."

"I keep telling you her illness is a disfiguring one; she won't meet strangers. And don't say you're not a stranger—you'd understand, but she's the one who wouldn't. Please don't nag me, Belsir."

"Sometimes I think you're a stranger, Balt," Embelsira declared emotionally.

"Yes, dear, I'm a stranger, anything you say, but let me get packed." He started folding a robe crookedly, hoping it would distract her into taking over the job.

But she leaned against the lintel, staring at him. "Balt, sometimes I wonder if you really have an aunt."

The only thing he allowed himself to do was put down the robe he was holding. "Do you think I send expensive toilet sets to myself? You must think Piq's right—I'm just plain crazy."

"Piq doesn't think you're crazy any more. He and the other old ones say you have a woman in Barshwat. But I don't believe that!"

"Maybe I do, Embelsira. A man's a man, even if he is a librarian."

"I know it isn't true. I think it's . . . something else entirely. You're so strange sometimes, Balt. How could somebody who comes only from the other side of the same world be so strange?"

*

He forced a grin. "Suddenly you've become very cosmic. What do you know of our—of the world? It's a big place. And nobody else in Katund seems to be so impressed by my strangeness; they think a foreigner's entitled to his queer ways."

"Nobody in Katund knows you as well as I do. And I've seen foreigners before. They're not different in the way you are." She looked intently at him. "It's not a shameful kind of strangeness, just a . . . strange kind of strangeness. Fascinating in its way—I don't want you to think I just married the first stranger who came along. . . . "

"I'm sure you had many offers, dear. Come, help me fold this cloak or I'll never make the bus."

"You know what I'm reminded of?" she said, coming forward and taking the cloak. "Of the old tale about the lovely village maiden who marries the handsome stranger and promises she'll never look into his eyes. And then one day she forgets and looks into his eyes and sees—"

"What does she see?"

"The worst thing of all, the greatest horror. She sees nothing. She sees emptiness."

He laughed. "The moral's clear. She shouldn't have looked into his eyes."

"But how can you help looking into the eyes of the man you love? Maybe that's the moral—that it was an impossible task he set her."

SENTRY OF THE SKY

"In those tales it's always the man's fault, isn't it? Not much doubt who made them up. Now, Belsir, please, I've got to finish packing. It'll be just my luck to have today be the day the bus to Zrig's on time."

"A couple of weeks ago I was in Zrig shopping and I saw an Earthman," she said, folding his cloak into the kit. "The way he walked, the way he moved, reminded me a little of you."

It was a long moment before he could speak. "Do I look to you like a dark-faced, dark-haired, brown-eyed—"

"I didn't *say* you were an Earthman! But if Earthmen can travel through the sky, they might be able to do other things, too; maybe even change the way a man looks."

He snapped the kit-fastener. "If you really believe that, you should be careful. Creatures as clever as that might be able to pluck your words from my brain."

"What if they did? I'm not ashamed. Or afraid, either."

He reached out and patted her arm. Maybe she wasn't afraid, but he was. For her. And for the people of Damorlan. If there was a deep-probe on the staff ship. . . . If only something could happen to him, so he could never reach Barshwat . . . Spano wouldn't know. He might guess, but he wouldn't know. He'd have to start all over again—and maybe things would turn out better next time.

*

General Spano and his secretary were waiting in Blynn's office. Clarey stretched out his foot in greeting, then recollected himself and reached out his hand. "You see, sir," he said with a too-hearty laugh, "I'm really living my part."

Spano beamed. "Damorlan certainly seems to agree with you, my boy. You look positively blooming. Doesn't he, Han?"

She nodded grave agreement.

The general sniffed. "What's that you two are smoking?"

"Marac leaves," Clarey said. "A native product. Care to try one?" He extended his pouch to Spano.

"Don't mind if I do," the general said, taking a roll. "Which part do you light? And why don't you offer one to Secretary Vollard?"

"Oh, sorry; I didn't think of it. The women here don't use it. Care to try one, Secretary?" As she took a roll, she looked at him searchingly. She was still beautiful in an Amazonian way, but he preferred Embelsira's way. He could never imagine Han Vollard warm and tender.

"Well, Clarey," Spano said, "you seem to be doing a splendid job. I've been absolutely enthralled by your reports." He settled himself behind Blynn's desk. "Pity the information's top secret. It could make a fortune on the tri-dis."

Clarey bowed.

"And those musictapes you sent back created quite a stir. We've brought along some superior equipment. The rig here is good enough for routine work, but we need better fidelity for this. And it would be appreciated if the colonel didn't beat time with his foot while you played—no offense, Blynn."

He turned back to Clarey. "Do you think you can pick up some of those what-do-you-call-'ems—ulerins—for us, too, or is there a tabu of some kind?"

"Not ulerins," Clarey corrected, "uleran. And you can walk up to any marketplace and get as many as you like—providing you have the cash, of course."

"I *told* you the job had musical overtones. I'll bet that makes up for some of the discomforts and privations."

"It's not too uncomfortable."

"There speaks a true patriot!" Spano approved.

Han measured Clarey with her eyes. "You're quiet, Secretary," he said nervously. "You used to talk a lot more."

Blynn stared at him. She smiled. "You're the one who has things to tell now, Clarey."

"And show," the general said, almost licking his lips. "Every one of your tapes made my mouth fairly water. I trust you brought an ample and varied supply of those delicacies."

Clarey's smile was unforced this time. "I got your message and I brought along a large hamperful, but it'll be hard to make the people back home keep thinking my aunt's an invalid if she eats like a team of hax. My wife baked some pastries, which I especially recommend to your attention."

"I think we ought to get business over before we start on refreshments," Han suggested.

"Yes," Spano agreed reluctantly. "I suppose you had better be deep-probed first, Clarey. . . . Not even one taste beforehand, Han? . . . Well, I suppose not."

Clarey tensed. "You've got a probe on the ship?" he asked, as if the possibility had never occurred to him.

"That's right," Han Vollard said. "It's an up-to-date model. The whole thing'll take you less than an hour, and we'll have the information collated by morning."

"I—I would prefer not to be deep-probed. You never can tell: it might upset all the conditioning I've received here; it—"

"Let us worry about that, Clarey," she said.

*

He didn't sleep that night. He sat looking out of the window, knowing there was nothing he could do. Embelsira was in danger—her people were in danger—and he couldn't lift a finger to save them.

When he came down to breakfast, he saw that the reports had been collated and read. "So your wife suspects, does she?" the general asked. "Shrewd little creature. You must have picked one of the more intelligent ones."

Clarey struggled on the pin. "Wives often have strange fancies about their husbands. You mustn't take it too seriously."

"How often have you been married, Clarey?" Han asked. "Or even linked in liaison? How many married people did you know well back on Earth?"

There was no need to answer; she knew all the answers.

"I think Clarey did a rattling good job," Blynn said stoutly. "It wasn't his fault that she suspects."

"Of course not!" the general agreed. "Feminine intuition isn't restricted to human females. In fact, in some female ilfs it's even stronger than in humans. The precognitive faculties in the grua, for example—"

"What are you going to do?" Clarey interrupted bluntly.

Han Vollard answered him: "Nothing yet. You've got us a lot of information, but it's not enough. You'll have to keep on as you are for another three years or so."

It was all Clarey could do to keep from trembling visibly with relief.

"It doesn't even matter too much that one of the natives suspects," Han went on, "as long as she doesn't definitely know."

"She doesn't," Clarey said, "and she won't. And she won't tell anybody; she'd be afraid for me." But he wasn't all that sure. The Damorlanti didn't hate Earthmen and they didn't fear them, and so Embelsira wouldn't think it was a shameful thing to be. He was glad he'd already been deep-probed. At least this thought would be safe for three years or so.

"At any rate, they don't seem antagonistic toward Earthmen," the general said, almost as if he'd read part of Clarey's mind. "I think that's nice."

Han Vollard looked at him. "It's not their attitude toward us that matters. They couldn't do anything if they tried. It's what they are that matters, what they will be that matters even more."

"I take back what I said before!" Clarey flared. "You talk too damn much!"

There was a chilling silence.

"Nerves," said Blynn nervously. "Every agent lets go when he's back among his own kind. Nothing but release of tension."

*

Several days later the staff ship was ready to go back to Earth. "Don't forget to tell your wife how much I enjoyed the pies," Spano said; then, "Oh, I was forgetting; you could hardly do that. But do see if you can work out something with the dehydro-freeze. I'd hate to have to wait three years before tasting them again. You can keep your marac rolls, though; I'll take my smoke-sticks."

"Try not to get any more involved, Clarey," Han Vollard said as they stood outside the airlock. "Maybe you ought to move on—to a city, perhaps, another country—"

"When I want your advice, I'll ask for it!" he snapped.

After they'd gone, Blynn turned on him. "Man, you must be out of your mind, talking to Secretary Vollard like that."

"Why does she have to keep meddling? It's none of her business—"

"None of her business! Secretary of the Space Service, and you say it's none of her business?"

Clarey blinked. "I thought she was Spano's secretary."

Blynn laughed until the tears dampened his dark cheeks. "Spano's only Head of Intelligence. She's his Mistress."

"Of course—*mistress*, feminine of *master*! I should have realized that before." Then Clarey laughed, too. "I'm a real all-round alien. I can't even understand my own language."

On the way back home he couldn't help thinking that Han Vollard might be right. It could be the best thing for him to disappear now; the best thing for himself, the best thing for Embelsira. He could pretend to desert her—better yet, Blynn could fake some kind of accident, so her feelings wouldn't be hurt. A pension of some kind would be arranged. She could marry again, have the children she wanted so much. If he waited the full ten years, she might never be able to have them. He had no idea at what age Damorlant females ceased to be fertile.

But she wasn't just a Damorlant female—she was his wife. He didn't want to leave her. Maybe he never would have to. Hadn't Spano said that when his term was over he could pick his planet? He would pick Damorlan.

*

When Clarey came home from Barshwat, Embelsira said nothing more about her suspicions, but greeted him affectionately and prepared a special supper for him. Afterward, he wondered if making love to an Earth girl could be as pleasant. He wondered how it would be to make love to Han Vollard.

The days passed and he forgot about Han Vollard. After much persuasion, he agreed to give a series of concerts at Zrig, but only on condition that Rini played with him and had one solo each performance. He was embarrassed at having so far outstripped his teacher, but Rini seemed unperturbed.

"My technique's still better than yours will ever be," he said. "It's this new style of yours that gets 'em. I understand it's spreading; it's reached as far as Barshwat. You should see the angry letters Irik writes about it!" Rini chuckled. "And he hasn't the least idea it started right here in his own home village that he's always sneered at for being so backward!"

Clarey smiled and clapped the boy on the neck. If it made Rini feel better to think Clarey had a new style rather than that Clarey played better than he did, Clarey had no objection.

Clarey was offered the post of head librarian at Zrig, but Embelsira didn't want to leave Katund, and, when he thought about it, he really didn't want to either. So he refused the job and didn't bother mentioning the matter to Headquarters.

As he grew more sure of himself and his position, he allowed his wealth to show. He and Embelsira moved into a larger dome. Instead of sending to Zrig or even Barshwat for the furnishings, they hired local talent. Tavan, the carpenter, made them some exquisite blackwood pieces inlaid with opalescent stone that everyone said was the equal of anything in Barshwat. A talented nephew of Hanxi's painted glowing murals; Embelsira's mother wove rugs and draperies in muted water-tones. The dome became the district showplace. Clarey realized he now had a position to keep up, but sometimes it annoyed him when perfect strangers asked to see the place.

He was invited to run against Malesor as headman but declined. He didn't want to be brought into undue prominence. Trouble was, as he became popular, he also aroused animosity. There were the girls who felt he should have married them instead of Embelsira, and their mothers and subsequent husbands. A lot of people resented Clarey because they felt he should have decorated his house differently, dressed differently, spent his money differently.

A man can live ignored by everyone, he discovered, but he can't be liked by some without finding himself disliked by others.

*

Matters came to a head in his fourth spring there. He thought of it as spring, although on Damorlan the seasons had no separate identities; they blended into one another, without its ever being very hot or very cold, very rainy or very dry. The reason he called this time of the year spring was that it seemed closest to perfection.

It was less perfect that year. Because it was then that Rini's brother Irik came back from Barshwat, after a six years' absence. He was very much the city man, far more so than anyone Clarey had seen in Barshwat itself. His tunics were shorter than his fellow villagers', and his cloaks iridesced restlessly from one vivid color to another. He wore a great deal of jewelry and perfume, neither of the best quality, and the toes of his boots were divided.

Clarey described this in detail to Embelsira the night Irik put in his first appearance at the Furbush. "You should have seen the little horror!"

"That's the way city men dress," Embelsira told him. "It's fashionable."

"But, dear, I've been to Barshwat."

"You don't have an eye for clothes. You never notice when I put on anything new. And I think it's unfair to take a dislike to Irik just because you don't care for the way he dresses."

"It's more than that, Belsira." And yet how could he explain to her what he couldn't quite understand himself, that Irik was vain, stupid, hostile; hence, dangerous?

"I swear to you, Balt," Embelsira said demurely, "that whatever there was between me and Irik, it all ended six years ago."

Clarey gave a start and then held back a smile. "I believe you, dear." And he kissed her nose.

*

SENTRY OF THE SKY

Irik held forth in the Furbush every evening of his stay in Katund. He had grievances and he aired them generously. He hated everything—the government, taxes, modern music, and Earthmen, whom he seemed to consider in some way responsible for the modern music, or at least its popularization. "Barbarians—slept completely through my concerts."

"But people are always falling asleep during concerts, Irik," Malesor pointed out reasonably. "And how could you expect barbarians to appreciate good music? What do you care for Earthmen's opinions as long as your own people like your music?"

Irik hesitated. "But the Earthmen have taken up the new kind of music; they stay awake during that. And—a lot of people seem to think that whatever's strange is good, so whatever the Earthmen like eventually becomes fashionable."

Hanxi wiggled his ears. "Fashions change. Well, who's ready to have his mug refilled?"

"But the Earthmen will keep on setting the fashions," Irik snarled. "Many people think the Earthmen know everything, just because they're aloof and have sky cars."

"Well," Malesor said, "the sky cars certainly prove they know something we don't. Better stick to your music, boy."

The smoky little bar-parlor resounded with laughter and Irik's face turned a nasty red. "They don't know anything about music and they don't know everything about machinery. We might surprise them yet. A friend of mine knows Guhak, the fellow who invented that new brake for the track car a few years ago."

"We know about that brake," Piq observed. "It stops a car so good, the chains are twice as late nowadays as they used to be, and you couldn't strictly say they were ever on time."

Everybody laughed again. Irik quivered with anger. "Guhak has invented a car that doesn't need to go on tracks. It can run *whenever* it wants *wherever* it wants. And one car will be able to go faster than three hax teams."

"That I'll believe when I've ridden on it," Kuqal grinned. "Even the chains aren't that fast." The others bit their thumbs and nodded—except Clarey, who was rigidly keeping out of the conversation. He forced squfur down his tightening throat and said nothing.

"You're backward clods!" Irik raged. "If the Earthmen can have cars that go through the sky without tracks why shouldn't we have cars that run on the ground the same way? Have we tried?"

"Doesn't seem to me it's worth the effort," Malesor said. "Our cars can get us where we're going as fast as we need to go already, why bother?"

"Whatever an Earthman can do, we can do better! Soon Guhak will get his ground cars on the road. After that, it'll only be a short step to cars that go in the sky. Then we'll find out where the Earthmen come from and why they're here. We'll be as powerful as they are. We'll get rid of them and their rotten music."

The bar parlor was silent, except for the clink as Clarey put his mug on the table. If he held it an instant longer, he was afraid he would spill it. One or two of the men looked at him uneasily out of the corners of their eyes. Malesor spoke: "In the first place, you don't know how powerful Earthmen are. In the second place, who wants to be powerful, anyway? The Earthmen haven't done us any harm and they're a good thing for the economy. My cousin in Zrig tells me one of 'em come into his store a coupla months ago and bought out his whole stock, every bolt of cloth. Paid twice what it was worth, too. Live and let live, I say."

The others murmured restlessly.

"If there are ways of doing things better," Rini suggested, "why shouldn't we have them, too?" His eyes darted quickly toward Clarey's and then as quickly away.

Irik turned his head and looked directly at Clarey for the first time. "You're silent, stranger. What do *you* think of the Earthmen?"

*

Clarey picked up his drink, finished the squfur and set the mug back down on the table. "I don't know much about Earthmen. An ugly-looking lot, true, but there doesn't seem to be any harm in them. Of course, living in Barshwat, you probably know a lot more about them than I do."

"I doubt that," Irik said. "You have an aunt in Barshwat."

Clarey allowed himself to look surprised before he said courteously, "I'm glad you find me and my family so interesting. Yes, it so happens I do have an aunt there, but she's rather advanced in years and doesn't enjoy hanging around the starship field the way the children do."

Irik's face darkened. "What is your aunt's name?"

This time everyone looked surprised. The question itself was not too out-of-the-way, but his tone decidedly was.

"She's a great-grandmother," Clarey said. "She would be too old for you. And I assure you it's difficult to part her from her money. I've tried."

Everybody laughed. Irik was furious. "I understand that your aunt lives very close to Earth Headquarters!"

Somebody must have followed him on one or more of his trips to Barshwat, Clarey realized. "If the Earthmen chose to establish themselves in the best residential section of Barshwat, then probably my aunt does live near them. She's not the type to leave a comfortable dome simply because foreigners move into the neighborhood."

"Perhaps she has more than neighborhood in common with Earthmen."

The room was suddenly very quiet again.

"She does sometimes go to sleep at concerts," Clarey conceded.

Irik opened his mouth. Malesor held up a hand. "Before you say anything more against the Earthmen, Irik," he advised, "you oughta find out more about them. Their cars move faster and higher than ours. Maybe their catapults do, too."

No one looked at Clarey. Malesor had averted a showdown, he knew, but this was the beginning of the end. And he had a suspicion who was responsible—innocently perhaps, perhaps not. Love does not always imply trust. And when he told Embelsira what had happened in the Furbush, she, too, couldn't meet his eye. "That Irik," she said, "I never liked him."

"I wonder how he knows so much about me."

"Rini writes him very often," she babbled. "He must have told him you were responsible for the new music. That would make him hate you. Rini likes to irritate Irik, because he's always been jealous of him. But the whole thing's silly. How could you possibly make over the world's music, even if you were—" Her voice ran down.

"An Earthman?" he finished coldly. "I suppose you went around telling everybody your suspicions, and Rini wrote that to Irik, too?"

*

"I didn't tell anybody!" she protested indignantly. "Not a soul!" She met his eye. "Except Mother, of course."

"Your mother! You might as well have published it in the District Bulletin!"

"You have no right to speak of Mother like that, even if it's true!" Embelsira began to sob. "I had to tell her, Balt—she kept asking why there weren't any young ones."

"You could've told her to mind her own business!" he snapped, before he could catch himself. Five years, and he still made slips. It was her business. On Damorlan, it was a woman's duty not only to have children but to see that her children had children and their children had children.

He made himself look grave and self-reproachful. "I have a confession to make, Belsir. I should have told you when I married you. I can't have children."

"I never heard of such a thing! Everybody has children—unless they're not married, of course," she added primly.

"It's an affliction sent by the gods."

"The gods would never do anything like that!" she declared confidently.

How primitive she is, he thought, and, then, angrily, how provincial I am! He had never stopped to think about it, but he knew of no married couple who had not at least one offspring; he and Embelsira were the only ones. It hadn't occurred to the X-T specialists that a species whose biological assets were roughly the same might have different handicaps. Apparently there was no such thing as sterility on Damorlan.

"Are you really an Earthman, then, Balt?" she asked timidly.

She had spread the news around, ruined him, ruined the work Earth had been doing, perhaps ruined even more than that—and she hadn't even been sure to begin with. But it was too late for recriminations. He had to salvage what little he could—time, maybe; that was all.

"Are you going to tell?" he asked.

She hesitated. "Do you swear you don't mean my people any harm?"

"I swear," he said.

"Then I swear not to tell," she said.

He kissed her. After all, he thought, it isn't a lie. *I don't mean her people any harm. Besides, sooner or later, her mother will get it out of her, so she won't be keeping her part of the bargain.*

*

The next time he went to Barshwat he knew he would be followed. He tried to shake the follower or followers off, but he couldn't be sure he'd succeeded.

He found the colonel looking out of the window with an expression of quiet melancholy. If there had been any Earthwomen on Damorlan, Clarey would have thought he'd been crossed in love.

"Things are taking a bad turn, Clarey," Blynn said. "There have been certain manifestations of hostility from the natives. Get any hint of it?"

"No," Clarey said, taking his usual chair, "not a whisper."

The colonel sat down heavily. "Katund's too out of the way. We should've moved you to a city once you'd got the feel of things. But you do go to Zrig occasionally. Haven't you heard anything there?"

"Only that an Earthman bought out a cloth merchant's entire stock at one blow."

Blynn grinned weakly. "Maybe it was rather an ostentatious thing to do, but the fabric's beautiful stuff."

He rubbed his nose reflectively. "Fact is, I've been hearing disturbing rumors. They say some fellow named Kuhak's invented a ground car that can run without tracks."

SENTRY OF THE SKY

Clarey almost said "Guhak," but caught himself in time. "Nonsense," he scoffed. "The more I know of them, the more surprised I am they ever got as far as inventing the chains."

"But they did, no getting around that. This is what Earth's afraid of, you know," he reminded Clarey—unnecessarily. "This is why you were sent here. And, if the rumor's true, it looks as if you weren't needed at all. I got the bad news by myself."

"But why should it be that upsetting?" Clarey tried to laugh. "You look as if it were the end of the world."

The colonel gave him a long, level look. "I consider that remark in the worst of taste."

Clarey stopped laughing.

"Remember," the colonel reminded Clarey, again unnecessarily, "this is the way we ourselves got started."

"But the Damorlanti don't have to move in the same direction. They may look human and even act human, but they don't think human."

The colonel clasped his hands behind his head and sighed. "There have been articles against us in the paper, and whenever we go out in the street people—natives, I mean—make nasty remarks and sometimes even faces at us. And what have we done to them? Carefully minded our own business, avoided all cultural contacts except for trade purposes, paid them much more than the going price for their goods, and gave them one or two tips on health and sanitation. As a result, they're beginning to hate us."

"But if you send a report, it'll bring the staff ship in ahead of time. Maybe the whole thing'll blow over. This way, you're not giving it a chance to."

The colonel chewed his lip. "Well," he finally said, "I might as well wait and see if the rumor's verified before I report it."

Clarey went back to Katund. The months went by. The friendly atmosphere in the Furbush had vanished, and not as many people stopped and chatted when they came to the library. But there wasn't any actual incident until the evening Clarey was walking home after late night at the library and a stone struck him between the shoulder-blades. "Dirty Earthman!" a voice called, and several pairs of feet scuttled off.

He didn't mention the incident to Embelsira, not wanting to worry her, but the next morning he went to the Village Dome and informed Malesor. "Very bad," the headman muttered. "*Very* bad. Whoever did it will be punished."

"You won't be able to catch them," Clarey said, "and there'd be no point in punishment, anyway. Look at it like this, Mal. Suppose I had been an Earthman, don't you see how dangerous this would be, not for me but for you? Can't you imagine the inevitable results?"

Malesor nodded. "The Earthmen's catapults do go farther and faster, then?"

"And maybe deeper," Clarey agreed, pretending not to notice that it had been a question. "After the way Irik talked, I couldn't help drifting over to the starfield when I was in Barshwat and watching an Earth ship come. You've no idea how incredibly powerful a thing it was. Anyone who has power in one direction is likely to have it in another."

"I wonder if the Earthmen always had power," Malesor mused, "if they weren't like us once. If, given time, we couldn't be like them. . . ."

Clarey didn't say anything.

Malesor's pale face turned gray. "You mean we might not be given time?"

SENTRY OF THE SKY

Clarey wiggled his ears. "Who can tell what's in the mind of an Earthman?"

Malesor looked directly at him. "Why do you tell me this?"

"Because I'm one of you," Clarey said stoutly.

Malesor shook his head. "You're not. You never can be. But thanks for the warning—stranger."

Never identify, the robocoach had said. *You'll never be able to become the character you're trying to play.* He was talking only of the stage, Clarey told himself angrily, as he left the Dome.

Reports trickled in from the cities. Earthmen had been stoned twice in Zrig, more often than that in Barshwat. Clarey got an agitated letter from his aunt. "Watch out for yourself, Nephew," she warned. "They may take it into their heads to attack all foreigners. Remember, come what may, you'll always have a home with me."

Then everything broke open. A group of natives attacked Earth Headquarters in Barshwat. The Earthmen sprayed them with a gas which made the attackers lose consciousness without harming them; that is, it was intended to work that way. However, one of them hit his head on the wall when he fell, and he died the next day.

The people of Vintnor were aroused. They milled angrily around Earth Headquarters carrying banners that said, "Go home, Earth murderers!" The headman of Barshwat called upon Colonel Blynn. The colonel courteously refused to withdraw his men from the planet. "I'm under orders, old chap," he said, "but I'll report your request back to Earth."

"It isn't a request," the headman said.

Colonel Blynn smiled and said, "We'll treat it as one, shall we?"

Clarey knew what happened, because the headman gave a report of the conversation to the Barshwat Prime Bulletin. He also got a letter from his aunt describing the incident as vividly as if she had been there herself. The Barshwat Prime ran a series of increasingly intemperate editorials calling upon all the nations of Damorlan to unite against the Earthmen; it was spirit that counted, it said, rather than technology. Malesor wrote a letter asking how superior spiritual values could compete against presumably superior weapons. He read it aloud in the Purple Furbush before he sent it to the editor of the Barshwat Prime, which was lucky, because the Prime never printed it, although the Dordonec Bulletin ran a copy.

*

However, the Barshwat Prime did print letters from editors in different countries. All of them pledged firm moral support. It also printed a letter from an anonymous correspondent in Katund which alleged that there was an Earth spy in that village, disguised as a Damorlant, and it was this spy who was personally responsible for the decline of musical taste on the whole planet. But the Bulletin seemed to consider this merely as an emanation from the lunatic fringe: "It would be as easy to disguise a hix as one of us as an Earthman. And, although we could certainly not minimize the importance of music in our culture, it is hardly likely that Earth would be attempting to achieve fell purposes through undermining that art. No, the decline in musical taste represents part of the general decline in public morality which has left us an easy prey."

Irik went back to Barshwat to help riot, but he left the Katundi convinced that Clarey was, if not actually an Earthman, at least a traitor. When he came into the Furbush, everybody got up and left. Nobody patronized the branch library any more. The constant readers went to the main library at Zrig, and, since the trip was expensive, their books were usually overdue and they had to pay substantial fines. Sometimes they never returned the books at all and messengers had to be sent from the city. Finally the chief librarian at

SENTRY OF THE SKY

Zrig issued a regulation that only those resident within the city limits could take books out; all others in the district had to read them on the premises. The Katundi blamed that on Clarey, too. One night they broke into his library and stole all the best-sellers.

A couple of days later, he came home and found all the windows of his dome broken. Best-sellers are often disappointing, he thought. He found a note from Embelsira, saying, "I have gone home to Mother."

He knew she expected him to go after her, but he wrote her a note saying he was going to see his aunt who was terrified by all the riots, and put it in the mail, so she wouldn't get it too soon. He packed his kit with his most important possessions and he took his ulerin under his arm.

When he reached Barshwat, he had some difficulty getting through the crowd in front of Earth Headquarters. All the windows were boarded up and the garbage hadn't been collected for a considerable length of time. Just as he reached the door, a familiar voice called, "That's the Earth spy!"

"Don't be silly!" another voice said. "He's obviously one of us!"

"But a traitor!" cried another voice. "Otherwise why go in there?" Stones splattered against the door, followed by impartial cries of "Spy! . . . Traitor! . . . Fool!" the last seemingly addressed to each other, rather than Clarey.

Blynn was haggard and anxious-looking "I've been wondering when you'd show up. Afraid maybe they'd got you—"

"I'm all right," Clarey interrupted. "But what are we going to do?"

Blynn laughed without stopping for a full minute. "Do? I'll tell you what we're going to do. We're going to sit tight and wait for the staff ship."

Two months later the staff ship came. Blynn radioed for the general and the secretary to come in a closed ground car.

"But why?" the general's voice crackled plaintively over the comunit. "I thought we didn't want them to know about ground cars—"

"They know," Blynn said crisply. "They've got one of their own now, maybe more. Crazy-looking thing, but it works. You'll see it outside Headquarters when you get here. The letters on the side mean 'Earthmen, Go!' Form imperative impolite emphatic."

Han Vollard strode into Headquarters, eyes ablaze. "Why didn't you send a report before trouble started? How could you allow an emergency situation to happen?"

Neither Blynn nor Clarey said anything.

"Very distressing thing," Spano declared. "Maybe it hit them so suddenly they didn't know it was building."

"You and Blynn get over to the ship right away for deep-probing," Han Vollard ordered, as both began to speak at once. "It's the only way I'll be able to get a coherent report."

After the results came through, her anger was cold, searing, unwomanly. "You knew a year ago that things were beginning to go wrong and you didn't even mention it on the tapes! I could have both of you broken for this."

"If only that were all there was to worry about," Clarey sighed wistfully.

*

She whirled on him. "Stop feeling sorry for yourself!" The sudden loss of control in that dark amazon was more threatening than anything that had happened yet.

"I'm not feeling sorry for myself," he said. "It's the Damorlanti I feel sorry for."

"You feel sorry for them because you identify with them. That makes you sorry for yourself."

She misunderstood his motives as she misunderstood everything he did or said, but their rapport wasn't at stake now. "What are you going to do?" he forced himself to ask.

"The decision will have to be made on Earth. Unless you mean what's going to happen to you? That's simple—you'll go back with us. Blynn will stay here, pending orders."

The colonel saluted.

"But I thought I was going to stay here ten years," said Clarey.

"Five to ten years," she corrected. "Apparently five was enough—" She cut herself short. "What's the matter with me?" she suddenly exclaimed. "I've been letting myself think in the same woolly way you do."

Suddenly, almost frighteningly, she smiled. "Clarey, you *did* the job we sent you out to do! You did it better than we expected! What threw me off was that we sent you out to act as an observer. Instead, you became a catalyst!"

She seized his hand and wrung it warmly. "Clarey, I apologize. You've done a splendid job!"

He wrenched his hand from her grasp. "I didn't act as a catalyst! It would have happened anyway." His voice rang in his own horrified ears—a voice begging for reassurance.

And she was a woman; she had maternal instincts; she reassured him. "It would have happened anyway," she said soothingly, "but it would have dragged on for years, cost the taxpayers billions."

"And now," he whispered, still unable to believe that the thing had really happened, "will you . . . dispose of everyone on Damorlant?"

She smiled and threw herself into a chair, her body limp and tired and contented-looking. "Come, Clarey, we're not that ruthless. Some kind of quarantine will probably be worked out. We just made the whole thing sound more drastic to appeal to your patriotism."

The general beamed. "So everything has worked out all right, after all? I knew it would. I always had the utmost confidence in you, Clarey."

She was busily planning. "We'll arrange some kind of heroic accident. . . . I have it! You died saving your aunt from the flames."

"What flames?"

"The flames of the fire that burned down her house. She died of the local equivalent of shock. Embelsira will be rich, so she'll want to believe the story. She'll be able to find herself another husband; she'll have children. She'll be better off, Clarey."

He looked at her, his misery welling out of his eyes.

"Oh, I don't mean it that way, man! All I meant was that you're a human being; she's not. I'm not saying one is better than the other. I'm saying they're different."

"But I felt less different with her, with the Damorlanti, than with anyone on Earth," he said.

She walked across to the window and looked out at the Damorlanti rioting ineptly below. "Most of us are happier in our dream world," she said at last, "but society couldn't function if we were allowed to stay there."

"Damorlan wasn't a dream world."

"But it will be," she said.

*

And so Clarey went back to Earth on the staff ship. Once its luxury would have given him pleasure; now the cabin with its taps that gave out plain water, salt water, mineral water, and assorted cordials held no charm; neither did the self-contained tri-di projector-receiver. The only reason he stayed there most of the time was to avoid the others.

However, he couldn't avoid turning up in the dining salon for meals. The greater his sorrow, the greater his appetite.

One day after lunch, Han stopped him forcibly, grasping his arm. "I've got to talk to you. Afterward you can go off and sulk if you want to. But we're going to make planetfall in a few days. It's necessary to discuss your future now."

"I have no future," he said.

"Come this way, Clarey. That's an order!"

Obediently, he followed her into a lounge that was a dazzle of color and splendor. There were eight pseudo-windows, each framing a pseudo-scene of a different planet at a different season. The harsh, barren summer of Mars, the cold, bleak winter of Ksud, the gentle green spring of Earth. . . . It must be a park, he knew; in no other place on Earth could spring be manifest—and yet it gave him a little pang to look at it. He tore his eyes away to turn them toward the others, and then up at the domed ceiling, fashioned to resemble a blue sky with clouds drifting across it. A domed ceiling . . . and he thought of the domes of Damorlan, light-years away among the stars. . . .

"I'm afraid the décor's a bit gaudy," Han apologized. "We didn't check the decorator's past performance until it was too late. But it's comfortable, anyway. Try one of these chairs. They accommodate themselves to the form."

She threw herself on a chaise lounge that accommodated itself perfectly to her form. She wasn't wearing her usual opulent secretarial garb, but something simple of clinging stuff that occasionally went transparent. So we're back to the first movement, Clarey though wearily.

He made sure that the chair opposite her was old-style before he lowered himself into it. "Where's the general? I thought he always sat in on these conferences."

"The formalities are over now," she said, smiling up at him. "Besides," she added, "if he doesn't take a nap after lunch, it wreaks havoc with his digestion. Afraid to be alone with me, Clarey?" she asked huskily.

"Yes," he said, rising, "as a matter of fact, I am, now that you mention it."

She sat up. "Sit down!"

He sat down.

She didn't recline again. Her dress went opaque, but her voice grew silken once more. "Listen, Clarey, I don't want you to think we're cheating you out of anything we promised. Even though you stayed only five years, you're going to have it all. You'll have U-E status—"

"What do I want that for?"

"Doesn't it mean anything to you any more, Clarey? It used to mean a lot, though you denied it even to yourself."

"Did it?" He forced his thoughts back through time. "I suppose it did. But I've changed. You know, those five years on Damorlan seem like—"

"Like a lifetime," she finished. "Couldn't we dispense with the clichés?"

"On Damorlan the things I said were fresh and interesting. On Damorlan I was somebody pretty special. I'd rather be a big second-hand fish in a small primitive puddle. Isn't there some way—"

"No way at all, Clarey! The puddle's drying up. We've got a nice aquarium ready for you. Why not dive in gracefully?"

"It was my puddle," he said. "I belonged."

*

SENTRY OF THE SKY

She closed her eyes and sank back into the chair which arched to meet the arch of her body. Lying down, she didn't look nearly as tall. "All right, let's give the whole opera one final run-through. Nobody cared for you on Earth; on Damorlan your friends liked you; your wife loved you. On Earth you never felt welcome and/or appreciated; on Damorlan you felt both welcome and appreciated. On Earth—"

He was stung out of his apathy. "That's right! I'm not saying I'm unique, only that I fitted—"

"How about trying to look at it from another point of view? Did it ever occur to you that, if the Damorlanti accepted you, so might your own people, if you approached them in the same way? Did you ever *try* to make friends on Earth?"

"But on Earth I shouldn't have to. They were my own people."

"Aha!" she cried gleefully.

"I mean—well, General Spano said it would be wrong to stoop to hypocrisy to win the friendship of my own people; that, if I did, their friendship wouldn't be worth anything. You can't buy friendship."

"You bought your ulerin. Does it play any the worse because you paid for it? Does it mean any the less to you?"

"What you're getting at," he said cautiously, "is that that's the way to make friends? By being a hypocrite?"

"Was it a sham with the Damorlanti?"

He had to stop for a moment before he could bring out an answer. "It started out as a sham—but I really got to like them afterward. Then it was real."

"So then you weren't a hypocrite, Clarey." Her voice grew more resonant. "Open yourself to people, show them that you want to be friends. Basically, everybody's shy and timid inside."

"Like you?" he said, casting an ironical glance at her dress.

70

"That's still the outside," she smiled, making no move to adjust it. "Listen to me, Clarey, and don't go off on sidetracks: The people of Earth are your own people. Your loyalties have always been with them."

She had almost had him convinced, but this he couldn't swallow. "If my loyalties had been with Earth, I would have sent back reports of the trouble. But I didn't. I tried to stop it from happening. There just wasn't anything I could do."

"The deep-probe never lies, Clarey. You didn't really try to stop it." She paused, and then went on deliberately: "Because you could have stopped it, you know quite easily."

"There was nothing I could have done," he stated. "Nothing."

"Remember the first time the staff ship came? Just before you left for Barshwat, the woman told you she suspected you were an Earthman. You were afraid for her. Do you remember that?"

He nodded. Yes, he remembered how terrified he had been then, how relieved afterward, thinking everything was going to be all right. Lucky he hadn't realized the truth, or he wouldn't have had those extra years of happiness.

*

Han went on remorselessly: "And you thought if only something would happen to you en route, she would be safe. We might guess why it had happened, but we couldn't know for sure. We'd have had to start all over again."

He couldn't move, couldn't speak, couldn't think. She spaced each word carefully, sweetly. "You were quite right. Because you were the only man on Earth, Clarey, who had the particular physical requirements and the particular kind of mental instability that we needed for the job. You just said you weren't unique, Clarey. You were too modest; you are. If you'd killed yourself then, your death would have served a purpose; you would have died a hero. Kill yourself now and you die a coward."

"But at least I'd be dead. I wouldn't have to live with a coward for the rest of my life."

"You're not a coward, Clarey," she said. "You wouldn't admit it, but you are and always have been a patriot. To you, Earth came first. It's as simple as that."

She had deep-probed his mind. She must know his true feelings. There was no gainsaying that. He could know only his surface thoughts; she knew what lay behind and beneath. And, he reminded himself, at the end the Damorlanti were actually turning on him.

"Try to think of the whole thing as a course in charm that you've passed with flying colors," she said.

"It seems rather an expensive way of making me charming," he couldn't help saying, with the last struggle of something that was dying in him, something alien that perhaps should never have been there in the first place.

"Whole civilizations have been sacrificed for nothing at all. This one will not be sacrificed, only quarantined. But its contribution could be of cosmic magnitude."

"Now what are you going to try to sell me?" he asked drearily. "Are you saying that the essence of the Damorlant civilization is going to live on in me, that I carry its heritage inside myself, and so I have a tremendous responsibility to the Damorlanti on my shoulders?"

She laughed. "You're really getting sharp, Clarey. If you stayed in the service, you could be one of our best operatives. But you're not going to stay in the service. Yours is a higher destiny. Here, catch!"

She tossed him something that glittered as it arched through the air.

It was a U-E identcube, made out in his name. He had only seen them at a distance, and now he was holding one warm and gleaming in his hand, with his name and his face in it. His face . . . and yet not his face.

"That's what you're going to look like when the plastosurgeons get through," she explained. "They'll pigment your eyes and skin and hair, and they may be able to add a few inches to your height. Though I think you actually have grown a little. Something about the air, or, more likely, the food."

"Embelsira thought I was handsome the way I was. Embelsira. . . ." But Embelsira was light-years away. Embelsira was part of a fading dream—and he was awakening now to reality.

"Look at the cube. Look at your status symbol."

He looked at it, and he kept on looking at it. He couldn't tear his eyes away. He was hypnotized by the golden glitter of it, the golden meaning of it. "Musician," he said aloud. "Musician. . . . " A dream word, a magic word. He hadn't thought of it for years, but this he didn't have to reach back for. Once touched on, it surged over him, complete with its memories.

*

But she had made it meaningless, too. He managed to tear a laugh out of his throat. "Spano said I'd be able to buy the Musicians' Guild when I had my million and a half. Apparently you've been able to bargain them down."

"This cost nothing except the standard initiation fee," she told him. "You came by it honestly—through your music, nothing else. And you have more than a million and a half credits, Clarey—nearly ten times that, with more pouring in' every day."

She touched a boss on the side of her chair and white light hazed around them. "I think we're close enough to Earth to get some of the high-power tri-dis," she said, "although we can't expect perfect reception."

Blurrily, a show formed—a variety show. At first it seemed the same sort of thing that he remembered dimly, more interesting now because it had almost the character of novelty. Then an ornate young man appeared and it took deeper significance. He was carrying a musical instrument—refined, machined, carefully pitched. He played music on the ulerin while a trio sang insipid Terrestrial words. "Love Is a Guiding Star" they called it, but that didn't matter. It was one of the tunes Clarey had taped.

She touched another boss. The blur reformed to a symphony orchestra, playing as background music to a soloist with another ulerin. "That's your First Ulerin Concerto," she said. "There are three more."

Another program was beginning, an account of the tribulations of an unfortunate Plutonian family. It faded in to the strains of ulerin music, to a tune of Clarey's. If they could have endured it to the end, she told him, it would have faded out the same way. "Every time they play it," she said, "somewhere on Earth a cash register rings for you. And this one's a daily program."

He watched transfixed and transfigured as program after program featured his music, his ulerin.

"Not just on Earth," Han said, "but on all the civilized planets, even in a few of the more sophisticated primitive ones. You're a famous man, Clarey. Earth is waiting for you, literally and figuratively. There'll be ulerin orchestras to greet you at the field; we sent a relay ahead to let them know you were coming."

But his mind was slowly alerting itself. "And where am I supposed to be coming from, then, since they're never to hear about Damorlan?"

"They've been told that you retired to a lonely asteroid to work—to perfect your art and its instrument."

Of course they couldn't divulge the truth about Damorlan. "It seems a little unfair, though," he said.

"Why unfair? After all, Clarey, the music is yours. You took Damorlan's melodies and made them into music. You took their ulerin and made it into a musical instrument. They're all yours, every note and bladder of them."

She reached over and put out a hand to him. "And I'm yours, too, Clarey, if you want me," she breathed. There was obviously no doubt in her mind that he did want her. And in his, too. One didn't reject the Secretary of Space.

He took the chilly hand in his. The skin was odd in texture. I'm imagining things, he thought. It's a long time since I touched a human female's hand.

"I must be a very important Musician," he said aloud.

*

She nodded, not pretending to misunderstand. "Yes, important enough to rate the original and not a reasonable facsimile. You're a lucky man, Clarey." And then she smiled up at him. "I can be warm and tender, I assure you."

It took him a moment to realize what she meant. For a moment he had that pang again. She would never be the same as Embelsira, but a man needed change to develop.

He was still troubled, though. "I want to do *something*. Even an empty gesture's better than none at all. The last few months, I started putting together a longer thing; I guess it could be a symphony. When I finish it, I'd like to call it the 'Damorlant Symphony.'"

"Why not?" she said. He thought she was humoring him, but she added, "They'll think you just picked the name from an astrogation chart."

In a final burst of irony he dedicated the "Damorlant Symphony" to the human race, but, as usual, he was misunderstood. In fact, one of the music critics—all of whom were enthusiastic over the new work—wrote, "At last we have a great musician who is also a great humanist."

Eventually Clarey forgot his original intent and came to believe it himself.